There's a DOG in my BRAIN

DOG SHOW
DISASTER

There's a DOG in my BRAIN

DOG SHOW DISASTER

Caroline Green

illustrated by Rikin Parekh

WALKER
BOOKS

First published 2022 by Walker Books Ltd
87 Vauxhall Walk, London SE11 5HJ

2 4 6 8 10 9 7 5 3 1

Text © 2022 Caroline Green
Illustrations © 2022 Rikin Parekh

This book has been typeset in Nimrod, Johann and Zalderdash

Printed and bound by CPI Group (UK) Ltd, Croydon CR0 4YY

British Library Cataloguing in Publication Data:
a catalogue record for this book is available
from the British Library

ISBN 978-1-4063-9944-8

www.walker.co.uk

For Freddie, who could give Dudley

a run for his money.

C. G.

For Bella and Nanu ... again. XX

R. P.

That was the **BEST DREAM EVER**.

There'd been a pile of delicious food in it.
And a ball. *A food ball!*

It looked like a regular ball but was made of
tangy cheese, with a hint of ham and a smidge of
sausagey loveliness.

Dudley sighs happily, sticking all four
legs out for a big stretch. But wait ... what's
this? Ears pricked, his nose begins to twitch.

7

Something yummy's going on. Maybe that's why he dreamed about food!

Padding into the kitchen, he thinks he's still dreaming for a moment because ...

... the table is *covered* with delicious things! There's a huge frosty cake, a towering pile of golden, jammy biscuits and a crinkly pie that smells like **DINNER**. Dudley puts his paws on the table to get a closer sniff.

Maybe one tiny lick of the big cake? Dudley very much wants to be a Good Boy. Would a Good Boy have a bit?

Definitely, he decides. Every Good Boy deserves cake.

LICK LICK.

Mmm, delicious!

Maybe one little nibble...

NIBBLE NIBBLE.

Perhaps one small chomp?

CHOMP CHOMP...

Dudley sighs happily. But the cake is all gone now. And Dudley is still hungry.

He eyes the rack of biscuits for half a second before gobbling one up. A bit hot, but deliciousness outweighs hot-ouchiness. So, like the very brave dog he is, he has another.

Then another.

Then another.

Until...

All gone.

Now there's only the dinner pie left...

For the next few minutes, Dudley munches away until...

ALL gone?

Nothing left but the icing on Dudley's sniffer, the pie crumbs stuck to his hearing flappers, and the jam on his paws. He lies down and starts licking the bits he can reach.

Then he hears...

"DUDLEY!!!"

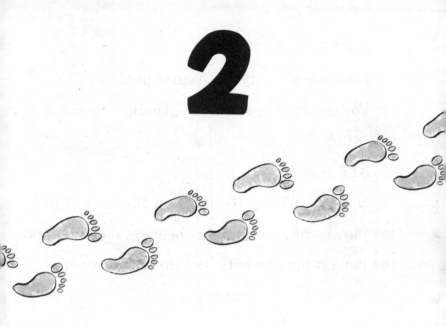

Danny is a coiled spring. He stretches a leg, flexes his toes.

This is it. His most daring jump yet. The leap from windowsill to bed wasn't for the faint-hearted, especially when he could fall on the various bits of discarded Lego or a crusty old plate on his bedroom floor.

Danny may be rubbish at football, but he's brilliant at climbing, jumping and balancing.

After watching parkour videos on YouTube,
he reckons he's found his sport. He hasn't told
anyone in case they laugh so, for now, he practises
only in his room.

Now!

He takes the leap ...

... as one very loud, very angry shout rings out.

"**DUDLEY!!!**"

One minute Danny's airborne and the next, he's on his bottom on the carpet.

Ouch!

But Dad sounds upset. Better go and investigate what's happening down there – bound to be Dudley-related.

Danny waits for a moment at the top of the stairs. Dad isn't quite done with the shouting yet.

"Go to your basket! And stay there!"

Dudley emerges from the kitchen and slinks across the hallway, hanging his head. Turning round three times in his bed, he flumps down, brown eyes under tufty dog-eyebrows worriedly searching for his friend Danny.

Danny hurries down, leaping over the last three stairs as usual. Dudley's tail begins to thump hard, mood instantly transformed, as if the very sight of Danny flicks a switch in Dudley's brain from Sad to Happy.

Crouching down, Danny scratches behind Dudley's silky ears and Dudley gazes up at him, eyes soft with doggy love.

"What have you been up to now then, boy?" Danny whispers, scratching harder so the dog gets a daft, blissed-out expression.

They both jump as the letterbox snaps open. A shiny piece of paper slips through, but before it hits the mat, Danny leaps forward and grabs it.

Yep, just as he suspected. It's *another* one of those flyers. It must be the third this week.

There's a photo of a man in mirrored sunglasses and another of a sleek, highly groomed dog with a snooty expression. In big letters it says:

DOGGY BOOT CAMP

Want to turn your delinquent dog into a perfect pooch?

Come along to Rex Power's Training for THE VERY WORST DOGS and transform their behaviour from slobbering loser to champion pet.

Very worst dog? *Slobbering loser?* OK, Dudley may be a bit slobbery, but he is the very **BEST** dog. Danny doesn't want him transformed. (Although he could live without with the slobber. And maybe the wind.) Anyway, Dudley *is* the best dog. Mum and Dad don't agree, though, which is why Danny has been hiding all the flyers before anyone can see them.

Crumpling the paper into his pocket, Danny kisses Dudley's soft, smelly head and then goes into the kitchen.

The first thing he sees is Dad dressed in his favourite apron (frilly and with "NO SOGGY BOTTOMS HERE" written on it), his face a worrying shade of purple. He's breathing hard.

The second thing Danny sees is that the table is covered in crumbs and smears of jam and cream. One of the best plates lies broken on the floor and the posh cake stand is on its side, rolling in gentle circles.

"*Just look* what that dog has done!" Dad clasps his head in despair. "Every single thing I painstakingly baked has been eaten! All that work!"

Danny tries to make a sound that combines sympathy and also "Don't be too cross with Dudley" all at once. He doesn't really pull it off.

Dad is obsessed with a TV show called "Britain's Best Bakers" and it has made him very competitive about his own efforts. Tomorrow it's the local County Fair and Dad is going to enter the baking competition. There's a rumour that the host of Britain's Best Bakers, Cressida Cruickshank, is going to be there. It's sent Dad into a baking frenzy.

The trouble is, he's not really very good at it. His pie bottoms are *always* soggy, his biscuits are so hard that Danny almost chipped a molar on one, and his cakes are so flat you could use them as Frisbees.

Only Dudley likes these efforts. In fact, it's fair to say he's the Number One Fan of Dad's baking. But when you think that Dudley has also eaten entire crisp wrappers, a remote control, a shuttlecock, many bananas with the skin still on *and* some fox poo, that isn't much of a compliment.

Mum comes into the kitchen and lets out a groan. "Don't tell me," she says. "Dudley?"

Dad nods miserably and sinks into a chair. A little bit of flour falls off his face as he puffs out his cheeks. He's always covered in a light dusting of flour, sugar or cocoa powder these days.

"He's eaten nearly the whole bloomin' lot," Dad says.

"That dog has gone too far this time," says Mum, turning to Danny. She starts counting on her fingers. "One, he broke a hole in the fence to chase a random cat. Two, he jumped on the sofa and shook so hard he redecorated the living room in mud. Three, he stuck his whole nose inside a little girl's bag of crisps in the park and made her cry. That was only in the last fortnight! And now this!" An ominous look crosses her face. "It's no good, Danny. There's only one thing for it."

She pulls a piece of paper out of her pocket.

"This came through the door when you were at school yesterday," she says. "Doggy Boot Camp! That'll sort him out!"

Dudley can't understand why he's been sent to his basket. There have been loads of times when the Dad says, "Come on, everyone, you have to help eat all these cakes! Guys...? Anyone?" But when Dudley helps? Oh no, it's a different matter.

He gives a big sulky huff and swipes his long pink tongue around his chops, hoping to find some stray crumbs. That's the trouble with doggy chops, he thinks. There's only so much food you can pick up in one go.

"Danny? Can you get that squashed bit of pie crust that's stuck under the cooker?" says the Mum from the kitchen.

See?

Then she says, "Darn it. I have jam on my slipper!"

Jam? Slippers? That sounds like a job for Dudley. He could lick it off and be the Good Boy again!

He clambers out of bed, tail like a fluffy arrow. Peering into the kitchen, he sees that the Mum, the Dad and Danny are all using their sausage paws to clear up the crumbs and wipe away the smears of delicious things.

Oh, how he wishes he had sausage paws too! It would be so great! Dudley wishes for this so hard his eyes go googly and his bottom makes a little PARP.

But what's this?

Something shivery passes through Dudley's head. He feels it fizz and whirl inside him ...

... down and down and down ...

... through his insides ...

... and right down to his paws.

It sounds like millions of dogs are barking all at once, inside *and* outside Dudley's head.

He lets out a low "WOOF?" because he's feeling decidedly un-Dudleyish all of a sudden.

As Danny turns away from putting crumbs in the bin, he tries to defend his dog once again.

"But Mum, Dudley isn't one of the very worst dogs! He's not a slobbery loser! Or a delinquent! He'll hate Boot Camp!"

"Oh, you've slunk out of your bed, have you?" says Mum, who's looking down on Danny from high up. "There's no need for that barking! You're still in our bad books, I'll have you know."

Huh?

What's going on? He looks around the kitchen and finds three faces staring back at him.

Mum's.

Dad's.

And his own.

His own?

Danny's head swims with confusion. Then he looks down to see a pair of hairy paws where his own socked feet should be and understands.

It's happened again. He's swapped bodies with Dudley!

Dudley, inside Danny's body, has entered the kitchen and is grinning goofily at everyone. And why is he doing that strange wiggling motion? *Is he trying to wag his non-existent tail?*

It's so embarrassing seeing himself like this. Danny would like to cover his face with his hands and hide. But he only has paws now.

He gazes up at Mum with desperation in his eyes. Mum looks back at him, crossly, seeing only Dudley. He takes the corner of her top in his mouth and gives it a little tug.

"It's *me*," he says. Or at least he tries to say it, but all that comes out is a growly sort of whine.

"What are you doing, Dudley?" says Mum, struggling to yank it out of his mouth.

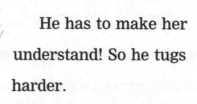

He has to make her understand! So he tugs harder.

She pulls back harder again.

"Dudley!" she shouts.

"Will you stop that? Haven't you had enough to eat already without going for my clothes too?"

This is hopeless!

But there's worse to come.

Dudley-as-Danny slinks past Mum and Dad with a very cunning look on his face.

Oh no.

"Danny! Why are you **LICKING MY SLIPPER?**" Danny has never heard such a high-pitched sound come out of Mum's mouth before.

Dudley may look like a boy, but his eyes say pure Naughty Dog.

"**STOP THAT!**" says Dad. "What are you *thinking*, Danny?"

Mum sinks into a chair and covers her eyes with a hand.

"I don't know what's happening in this house," she says. "We have the world's worst dog and a child who sees him as a role model."

This is an emergency! If Danny doesn't swap back **RIGHT NOW**, they're doomed!

He closes his eyes and wishes as hard as he can, with every little molecule of his being.

Come on, swap us back, he thinks. *I wish, I wish, I wish we could swap back...*

But nothing happens.

The funny tingly feeling has gone, which is good. But there's a funny-looking dog in Dudley's kitchen, which is bad.

And then the Dad pulls the scary-bendy-tube monster from the cupboard in the kitchen and says, "I'd better vacuum up the rest of this," which is **VERY BAD INDEED**.

Dudley hurries into the hallway to the safety of his bed.

But that Other Dog follows him out of the kitchen. Does he *know* this dog? Dudley goes to give his bottom a sniff. Nothing. Hmm ... maybe his sniff has got broken again?

It's only now he notices the sausage paws, just like he wished for. Although he's not really sure what to do with them now that all the cake has gone!

The Mum comes into the hall. "What the heck are you *doing*, Danny?"

Huh? Dudley turns around. No Danny there. He goes into the hall and peers up the stairs. No Danny there either. Where *is* Danny?

"I'm going to pretend I didn't see that," says
the Mum in a funny voice, her eyes big circles.
"Anyway, it's all decided. The Doggy Boot Camp
starts in an hour."

The doorbell rings and there's a shape at the
glass window that appears to be throwing a ball
up and down. Today just got better! Maybe the
ball will be made of food, like in the Best Dream
Ever?

"Oh hello, Priya!" says the Mum, opening the
door.

"Hi, Aunty Annie," says the Priya. "I'm on
my way home from football practice and thought
I'd say hello. What's up, Danny?"

All this Danny talk but no Danny! But Dudley
decides not worry about that and watches the
ball go *up, down, up, down, up, down,* in the
Priya's hand.

"Maybe you can talk some sense into him,"
says the Mum. "He and Dudley are as bad as

each other. Now if you'll excuse me, we're just clearing up the latest bit of Dudley destruction."

She walks off.

"Hmm," says the Priya, looking down at that Other Dog. "What have you been up to now, Dudders?"

Why is she calling that dog the special Dudders name? She's not even looking at him!

The Other Dog whines and pats her with its paw, but Dudley can't take the whole up-down thing with the ball for a moment longer. He launches himself at it and the Priya collapses in a heap on the floor under him.

"Oof!" she says. "You nearly squashed me!"

The funny dog is nudging at her with his nose and whining.

"Are you trying to tell me something, Dudders?" she says.

The Priya goes very still and looks into the dog's eyes, her hands on each side of his head.

The dog isn't wagging his tail, which is, quite frankly, rude.

"No," she mutters. "Don't be daft, Priya."

Dudley's licking the tennis ball now. It definitely doesn't taste of cheese or ham and there isn't the slightest hint of sausagey loveliness. In fact, it tastes awful. He tries to gnaw it instead but his teeth aren't bitey enough any more.

Then the Priya comes over to Dudley and takes his head in her hands. When he tries to lick her face, she gives a tiny shriek and lets go of him.

"Something's going on, isn't it?" she says.

The Other Dog barks twice, then races up the stairs. He comes back with Danny's T-shirt in his mouth. The cheek! It's *Danny's*.

Dudley tries to pull it away with his mouth but had forgotten about his not-sharp teeth. The Other Dog growls and hangs on tightly.

"OK, stop!" says the Priya. "Are you trying to give me a message, Dudley?" Her eyes go wide. "Has it happened again?"

The Other Dog whines, then nods its head up and down very fast.

"You *are* trying to tell me something, aren't you ... *Danny*?"

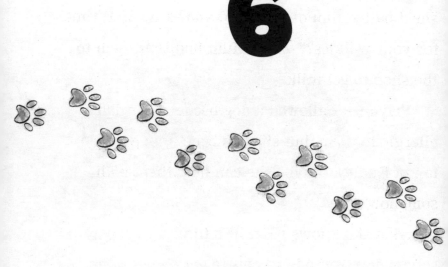

6

"*PHEW!*" says Danny, but of course all that comes out is "*WOOF!*"

Priya gets it!

Swapping bodies happened once before, but Danny never told *anyone*. Even so, Priya seemed to know something had happened from the way she behaved around Danny afterwards. Sometimes she would point at him and say, "SIT" before dissolving into giggles when he looked confused. And take last weekend, when she'd patted him on the head and said, "Is it time for your walkies?" when Mum had sent them to the shop to get milk.

Priya isn't allowed a dog because her dad's allergic to them, but she has been a long-time fan of Dudley. Maybe she can help them both somehow?

As if she knows what he's thinking, Priya squats down onto her heels to get close to him again and says, "Are you Danny? Paw the ground once for yes, twice for no."

Danny paws the carpet once, carefully.

"Blimey," she says, sitting back against the wall. "I knew it!"

She ruffles the top of Dudley's head with a laugh, which is so strange to see it almost makes Danny's brain explode. He wants to go, "Oi! Leave me alone!" but he can't. It's not *his* head right now but it still feels wrong.

And Dudley, the traitor, rewards her with a big dopey grin and – ugh! – a lick of the hand.

"Ugh!" Priya snatches her hand away, looking a bit green.

Dudley did that but *Danny* is the one who resolves to gargle with mouthwash once he gets his boy-body back. Who knows what else Dudley might lick?

Mum bustles back into the hall.

"Can't stop, Priya. I have to take Dudley to Doggy Boot Camp. If this doesn't improve his behaviour, I might have to sell him on eBay."

What?!

Danny gives Priya a desperate look and paws at her foot.

"Oh!" says Priya, then, "I reckon he'll smash that!"

"*Smash* it?" says Mum in horror.

"No, no," says Priya hurriedly, looking down at Danny with an eyebrow raised. "I mean, pass with flying colours!"

Hmm ... she's right. Maybe this isn't such a bad idea after all. Danny will go to Boot Camp and show how perfectly behaved one dog can be. Maybe he'll get a special certificate! He can produce it whenever Dudley is naughty.

Perfect pooch? Champion pet?

Oh yes.

That's exactly what he, Danny Pond, is going to be.

"But why don't *we* take him?" says Priya. "Me and Danny? Danny looks, er, like he could do with some fresh air..."

Danny looks over to see Dudley staring into the hall mirror so closely that he bumps his nose and yelps. Except, of course, it is *Danny's* body standing there and *Danny's* nose. No wonder Dudley looks confused.

Before Mum can react, Danny rushes to pick up the lead from the bottom of the coatrack, then waits expectantly by the front door.

Priya grabs the lead.

"Look how keen he is!" she says. "We'd better not hang on a moment longer!"

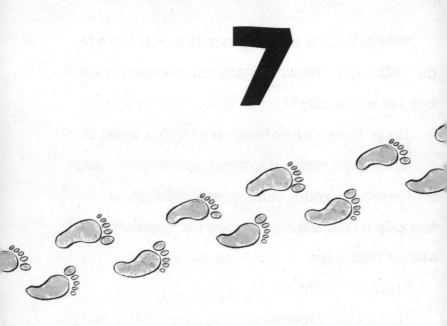

7

Dudley is out on the street but the Other Dog is wearing his lead.

It's nice being free but **THE OTHER DOG IS WEARING HIS LEAD!** Which is plain wrong. They get round the corner and the Priya says, "Right, come here, Dudders."

She unclips the lead from the Other Dog and attaches it to Dudley's middle, where the funny cloth things on his leggies start.

"No collar, so your trouser belt will have to do," she says. "Now, are you going to be a good boy for us, Dudley?"

He is! Doesn't he always try to be a Good Boy?

They walk down the street and Dudley spots a promising-looking lamp post. He swerves towards it, pulling the Priya with him so she almost falls over.

"Hey!"

Dudley isn't listening.

Hmm, this lamp post doesn't smell right...

Still, maybe he'll just...?

He has only managed to *half* cock his leg when the Priya yanks him back towards her.

"Oh dear!" she says. "We can't have that, Dudders. Just stay close, OK? Heel!"

Dudley gives her a grumpy look and turns to see the Other Dog has stuck his head inside a hedge. Maybe there's something nice to eat in there?

"Come out, Danny!" says the Priya, making snorty laughing noises. "There's no point in hiding! We have to get through this!"

Huh? Why do people keep saying "Danny" when Danny isn't here? There's only that strange dog wearing Dudley's collar. Where *is* Danny? Dudley misses Danny.

Dudley gives a sad sigh and lets himself be

pulled along by the middle. Every time he tries to sniff a lamp post or pick up a lovely banana skin from the pavement, the Priya yanks him closer.

These are *rotten* walkies. Worst ever!

"Come on, lads!" says the Priya, making those snorty noises again. "Heel! Both of you!"

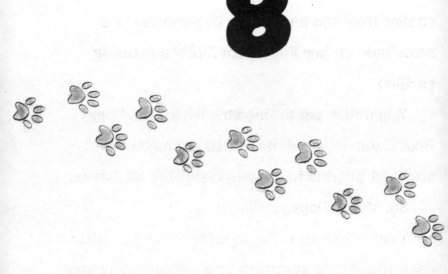

HEEL? What a cheek.

Danny thinks Priya might be enjoying this a bit too much. Dudley is being so embarrassing!

Luckily Danny is now distracted by a waft of fish and chips. Must be coming from the chippie on the nearby high street.

His doggy-nose is already twitching at the bombardment of pongs drifting up from the pavement, the hedges, the houses and even Priya (apple shampoo, tomato soup from her lunch, rubber from the tennis ball in her hand and some mud on her knee from football training earlier).

When they get to the park where the Doggy Boot Camp is based, it feels like someone has attached weights to his paws, slowing him down.

So. Many. Dogs.

They all seem to be in motion. One, a little Jack Russell, is spinning in a circle on the spot and barking, apparently trying to eat its own tail. A German shepherd lunges at everyone who walks past and almost pulls over the tiny blonde-haired woman holding its lead. A golden cockapoo is yapping loudly and attempting to climb up the leg of an elderly man with a moustache and grumpy eyebrows. "Down, Basil, down!" he keeps saying but the dog ignores him.

When the other dogs see Danny they stop

and stare at him as one. Then they all erupt into furious barking. It's a cacophony of canine sound. A couple look as though they would quite like to eat him. This really is the School for Bad Dogs. All the reprobates are here. These Naughtiest of the Naughty Dogs know there is something not quite right, not quite doggy enough about him. And do they mind? Oh yes they do.

Dudley isn't exactly going unnoticed either. A Rottweiler with a massive square head and a set of teeth like a *T. rex* snarls and pulls, trying to get closer, snapping and drooling. Dudley responds by leaping into the arms of a barrel-chested man with a one-eyed poodle at his feet. The man cries "Hey!" and drops him immediately.

It's as if Danny and Dudley don't make one proper dog between them. And the proper dogs know.

The Rottweiler lunges towards Dudley again. Danny has to do something!

Even though he'd like to run away extremely fast, Danny forces himself to stand in front of the angry dog and bark back.

Dudley cowers behind him. Danny barks and barks.

The Rottweiler is so shocked it does
nothing for a moment, but the other dogs sense
something and begin to form a circle around
Danny, Dudley and Priya. The big dog snarls
and lowers its body to the ground, just about to
strike...

Then a piercing whistle cuts through the
air and a familiar-looking man, with shoulders
as wide as an armchair, strides over to the
assembled group.

"What have we got here!" he yells. "Who
does THIS bad dog belong to?" He points a finger
down at Danny.

Bad dog?

"Um," says Priya, "he's with me, but he's not
really bad, he just—"

Ignoring her, the man stands in front of the
group, scowling, hands on hips.

Rex Power looks exactly like the photo on
the flyer. He has close-cropped hair like an

Action Man and, under a camouflage jacket, he's wearing a green vest, with *Rex Power: Extreme Dog Trainer™* written on it. He has combat trousers and big army boots and his eyes are hidden behind mirrored sunglasses.

A very slender and elegant Afghan hound with silky hair and a snooty expression stands next to him, regarding the other assembled dogs – including Danny – with a disapproving swish of the head.

Even from where he's standing, Danny catches Rex Power's strong smell. It's a funny mixture of leather, engine oil, sweat and other things Danny can't name, but the combination immediately makes him want to be ... smaller. He can feel the hairs rising along his back. Danny has seen this happen to Dudley when bossier dogs were around and now he knows why. Rex Power quite simply smells like he's **IN CHARGE**.

"Right, you lot!" the man bellows. "I'm Rex Power! And this is Princess Fenella, my beautifully behaved thoroughbred Afghan hound. This dog is an example of canine perfection! Every single one of you has come here today because you have an inferior dog to Princess Fenella. An inferior dog *you* can't handle. If you want to see what perfection really looks like, come and watch us compete at the County Fair dog show tomorrow. You can see for yourselves what your dog will be like, once they have been through my intensive training."

"I've heard there's a big cash prize for the

winner at that show," whispers the poodle owner to Priya. "Five hundred pounds!"

Priya looks down at Danny, eyebrows raised. But Danny is being stared down by the Rottweiler, who has a string of drool hanging from its chops, clearly imagining the lovely meal to come. And Dudley is using Priya as a human shield, hands over his face, as though this makes him invisible, like Danny believed when he was three.

Danny swallows.

Prize money? Who cares? If he and his dog can get through this without being eaten alive, he'll take it as a win.

"So let's make one thing clear," Power continues. "Your dog isn't the boss. Who's the boss?"

Silence.

"Um, you are?" says the elderly man.

"**NO!**" bellows Rex Power. "*You are!* Now get ready to rumble. There's work to be done!"

9

Dudley tries to wag his tail to show he wants to play, but none of the other dogs seem to like him. He knows this even without his sniff.

It's not that he wants to be Top Dog. (Dudley is never Top Dog.) He just wants to *play*, especially with the tiny one next to him, but she's showing her teeth and growling. Dudley knows what he has to do to prove he's not Top Dog. He'll make himself very ...

... small.

But when he lies down, trying to curl up, nose to tail, the Priya hisses, "Get up!" like he's done something wrong!

A man says, "What an unusual boy."

Unusual Boy? Maybe that's like Good Boy?

"What's happening over there?" shouts the Man with Shiny Eyes. "I see you are getting distracted by your boyfriend when you should be paying attention to me!"

"Boyfriend?! He's not my boyfriend!" says the Priya, teeth bared just like a dog. Then she turns

to Dudley and speaks very slowly and quietly.
"Dudley," she says, "you're making things worse.
Now if you go and chase the ball and *wait exactly
where it lands*, I promise you will be the Best
Boy Ever, OK?"

Dudley only registers the most important
words there: "ball" and "best boy". Things are
looking up!

"Sorry, everyone," she says, then throws
the ball a long way away from all the dogs and
humans. There's a frenzy of barking and all
the dogs try to get away, some of them pulling
their owners off their feet. But Dudley isn't on a
lead! He's free! He bounds away across the grass
to where the ball lands and picks it up in his
mouth, before remembering how bad it tastes.

Hmm...

There's lots of shouting over where the Priya
and the Other Dog are standing, but no one is
looking at Dudley any more.

He's getting a fizzy feeling, like he wants to wag his tail even though it's not there.

It feels like *fun*...

Dudley wants to be the Best Boy. Doesn't he? Definitely. But the waggy tail feeling is getting stronger.

No one is looking at him. He's not on the lead.

He could do **ANYTHING!**

That's when he gets a very clever idea that makes him wag his non-tail for real. He'll go for walkies by himself and find Danny!

10

So far at Doggy Boot Camp, Danny has practised:

• Sitting.

• Standing on one spot until called.

• Standing close when the human says "Heel".

The owners have mainly practised being shouted at by Rex, who yells, "Who's the boss?" roughly every minute and a half. This is followed by a feeble chorus of "I am" that fools no one.

Only Priya is replying with gusto. Danny is going to have words once this is over. Like she's the one who deserves the credit when he is the one doing all the good stuff! All he wants is to survive this class, get the certificate and be able to prove that Dudley is a good boy after all.

But where *is* Dudley? Danny hasn't seen him since he ran off after the ball and very much doubts the dog is waiting patiently where Priya told him to.

He doesn't get time to worry further because Rex Power is blowing an extraordinarily loud whistle. (That's what he does when he's not yelling.)

"We're going to do the assault course now," he says. "Dogs usually misbehave because they're bored. Come with me!"

Everyone follows him – some people being dragged by their barking or yapping dogs – to an area where he has set out a series of obstacles in

bright colours, with REX POWER – EXTREME
DOG TRAINER™ written on a big banner tied
between some trees.

There are various jumps to be navigated,
including a long tunnel, a kind of seesaw and
even a small trampoline. Danny feels his ears
pricking up and his tail wagging all by itself. This
is more like it! Like parkour for pooches! And no
one will be able to laugh at him because all they
will see is a dog getting some exercise.

"**RIGHT!**" yells Power. "I am going to show
your dogs how this is meant to be done. Princess
Fenella, come!" He clicks his fingers and the
Afghan hound trots over with her head held high,
coat shining in the afternoon sun like golden silk.

Danny swears she gives him the snootiest
look of all the dogs, even though he's the only
one not barking up a storm, spinning in a circle,
or attempting to lunge at another dog. One huge
St Bernard has pinned its owner to the ground, a

small woman in a beanie hat with a sad face who keeps saying, "Up, Tinkerbell. UP."

Princess Fenella goes to the start of the assault course and waits as Rex Power holds up a hand. He drops it swiftly and blows the piercing whistle at the same time. *Ouch*, thinks Danny. These ears really need a bit more respect.

Princess Fenella is OFF.

She zooms through the tunnel at the start, then neatly weaves in and out of some tall cones, her body a slinky S-shape. Stepping

carefully onto the seesaw, she effortlessly trots
up and stops dead centre, looking smugly at
her audience, before walking down the other
side as easily as if she were strolling down the
pavement. When she gets to a high beam with
a slope at each end, she climbs up and gives
herself a shake at the top, as if to say, "Look how
easy this is for me!" Then she sashays back down
in her own time.

There's lots of *ooh-ing* and *aah-ing* from the dog owners at this, and even some of the dogs look impressed, including a completely circular pug, who stops barking for the first time since they all arrived.

Before her grand finale, Princess Fenella struts around the perimeter of the course, then stands a few paces away from the trampoline. But wait, what's this? She randomly starts barking and turning in circles. It's like she's had enough of being perfect or something.

Someone says, "Oh dear."

Rex Power hurries over to his dog. Kneeling down in front of her, so his wide shoulders block the view, he reaches into his pocket and then does something Danny can't see. Gives her a treat perhaps.

When he gets up again, Princess Fenella is back to her well-behaved self.

She pauses, her entire body poised and

still like an arrow about to be fired. Then she lunges at the trampoline, an arrow of doggy determination. Jumping onto it, she bounces once in the air and then lands neatly on all fours on the other side.

The dog owners all erupt into riotous applause.

"Perfection! Like I said!" Rex Power's face is a picture of pride. "Now which dog dares to go next?"

I do, thinks Danny. *I'll show you, Princess Smugpants.*

GAME ON.

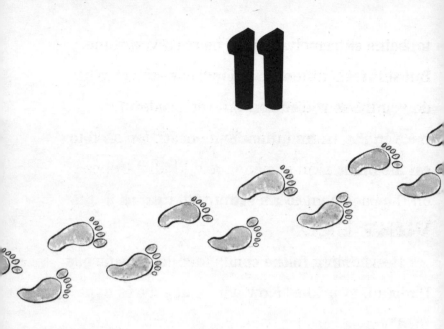

11

No matter how hard Dudley sniffs, he can't find Danny. He can't work out whether this is because Danny isn't here, or because his sniff is broken.

The fact is, *nothing* smells right. Not a single lamp post. (Dudley has tested every single one on the way.) Not the various bushes, not the bus stop, not even that man's trousers.

Humans keep staring at him, which he's used

to, being extremely handsome and everything. But this feels different. One woman said, "What do you think you're doing?" very rudely.

Nothing tastes quite right either. He tried to eat a banana skin someone had kindly dropped on the pavement to cheer himself up and it was **VERY BAD.**

He's coming to the conclusion that being Not Dudley is Not That Exciting.

Then he sees he is near a Good Place! It's where the Dad buys the newspaper Dudley Must Not Chew and sometimes stops to get sausage rolls from the Yummy-Pongs Place next door. Danny feeds Dudley bits of sausage roll as they walk home, whispering, "Shh, boy, don't let Dad see."

It's over *there* but there are lots of the horrible vroom-vroom machines in the way.

Dudley steps out into the road.

SCREEEEECH!

He opens one eye to see a vroom-vroom machine close up.

"Be careful, young man!" says a nice lady, taking him by the paw and leading him across the road.

Dudley is so happy to be safely in the Good Place that he tries to press up against her leg for a head rub. But she pulls a funny face and hurries away.

He turns his attention back to where he is. There are quite a lot of Fun Things to do here. The first Fun Thing is that he can see lots and lots of newspapers to chew *and there's no one here to tell him not to*.

With an excited feeling in his tummy, Dudley picks a newspaper and gives it a cautious chew. Hmm. Bit dry. But better than the banana skin. He chomps on a mouthful more before letting it fall to the street. Better try another.

Soon there is a big shredded newspapery pile

at his feet. Did he really chew so many? He looks around in case there is another dog, but nope. Just Dudley.

A loud **HISSSSS** behind makes him turn around. It's another Fun Thing. A bendy water snake!

Mum uses one of these in the garden! They play a game where she sprays him and Dudley tries to bite the water, barking up a storm.

The human is spraying the pavement but must really mean it for Dudley. So he bounds over and tries to bite the arc of cold water, then the bendy tube itself.

"Oi!" says the man. "What are you doing, you naughty boy? You've broken my hose! Clear off!"

Dudley whines and tries to flatten his ears. Naughty Boy is like Bad Boy.

He slinks away, looking around, ears still flat. Or at least, flat in his mind.

No Danny.

No more Fun Things.

But then Dudley stops dead. He can feel all the fur on his head standing to attention.

A big white vroom-vroom machine is outside the Sausage Roll Place! The back is all open and no one is there.

And inside the back? Not just one sausage roll! Not just whatever-comes-after-one sausage roll! **A WHOLE WORLD OF SAUSAGE ROLLS!**

12

Danny shoots through the bendy tunnel at top speed, barely touching the sides as he goes. Next, he jumps onto the seesaw and makes it across without a single wobble. The crowd is beginning to murmur a bit now. Someone even lets a little whoop of excitement.

They're loving him! He's even better than Princess Smugpants.

Danny climbs up onto the high bar and does

a perfect prance across, even turning around on the top.

This is **BRILLIANT!** He's like an amazing parkour star in doggy form. He's not even the slightest bit nervous about everyone watching, like he would be in his real body.

But the best is still to come: the trampoline. Trampolines happen to be one of his favourite things in the world and he is very good at backflips.

But that's in his boy body. Can he do this properly in Dudley's? Maybe he should be nervous? But wait ... Dudley never has doubts like these. He just gets on with it!

Danny glances over at the crowd, which seems to have grown to include some random passers-by. He bounces onto the trampoline. It feels like his boy-brain is telling his doggy body exactly what needs to be done. He bounces once, bounces twice ...

... and does a perfect backflip before landing on all four paws to thunderous applause.

Grinning, he jumps off the trampoline, his tail going so fast it's almost wagging him off his feet.

Not everyone is impressed though. Rex Power and Princess Fenella wear identical stony expressions.

"Hmm," says Power, stroking his dog's head. "I think that was clearly a bit of a fluke, so we'll move on quickly—"

"Wait," says Basil-the-cockapoo's owner, holding up a finger. "Don't you think that Dudley should enter the dog show tomorrow? I mean, he's *awfully* good."

A few people murmur agreement.

"Yeah, he's a bit of a superstar," says someone else.

Another voice says, "Reckon that dog could win the five hundred quid with skills like those!"

Rex Power is as still as a statue, his face unreadable behind his sunglasses.

Priya looks down at Danny.

Danny looks up at Priya.

No ... he couldn't. Could he? Take part as Dudley? Bit risky. Mind you, winning that money – as Dudley – could be just the thing to make Mum and Dad happy with the dog again—

"Of course," says Power, interrupting his thoughts. "Princess Fenella isn't scared of a bit of competition. No true champion is. Well, maybe I'll see you there then, Dudley."

And he looks at Danny in a way that makes his fur creep from head to tail.

13

All the way back the Dad shouts:

"Four hundred pounds of damage?"

And,

"What were you *thinking*?"

Then,

"I'll never be able to show myself at football
again. I bet Mike from the shop will tell everyone
what my naughty son did!"

Dudley trots very close next to him so he

doesn't get into any more trouble. He wants to give the Dad's hand a big lick to say sorry, but something tells him it's not the right time.

His mind keeps churning over all the Things. The Good Things, like the newspapers, the bendy water tube, the sausage rolls. Then all the Bad Things. The *shout-shout-shout* and *"No! No! No!"* from a man with a red face.

Red Face Man had said, "I know who you are, my lad! I play football with your dad. I'm going to ring him right now!"

The Dad arrived really fast after that. And his face was even crosser.

When they get into the house, Dudley climbs onto the sofa and curls himself as small as he can be. But it doesn't stop all the shouty crossness.

The Mum says, "How on Earth did you cost us *four hundred pounds*? For a couple of newspapers and a sausage roll or two?"

The Dad says, "It was a *huge pile* of newspapers and an *entire tray* of posh sausage rolls from the fancy farm shop. You know how expensive they are! Plus he knocked down half the display and smashed a shelf of home-made chutneys. Oh, and did I mention he bit the brand-new power hose Mr Singh from the grocery shop was using to clean the pavement!"

The Mum puts her face in her hands. "Danny, Danny, Danny," she says. "What were you *thinking*? You were supposed to be with Priya and Dudley!"

Dudley still doesn't know why people keep talking about Danny when he isn't here. But he is so happy to hear his *own* name, he barks "DUDLEY!" and gets out of bed to run in a circle.

Round and round and round he goes ...

... until he falls in a heap, panting, on the floor, grinning up at the Mum and the Dad.

They don't say anything at all. They only stare down at him with big, wide eyes.

14

Where's Dudley?

The people and their dogs are all starting to drift home but there's no sign of him.

Danny feels terrible for enjoying himself. Where's his dog? And just as importantly, where's his own body?

They frantically search the park in vain.

Danny gets an idea and starts to run towards the gate.

"Wait! Where are you going?" cries Priya, rushing after him. "We can't go home yet!"

Danny barks and points his nose in the direction of home.

At first she looks confused, but he barks some more and thankfully she seems to get it.

"OK!" she says. "Let's see if he's already there!"

When they get back, Danny is relieved to see his own boy form curled up in the dog bed, even if it looks strange. And even if Mum and Dad are staring at that boy form with very funny looks on their faces.

"Um, is everything OK?" says Priya.

"It's Danny," says Dad.

"He ate all the sausage rolls," says Mum, baffled. "And broke Mr Singh's hosepipe. Cost us four hundred pounds."

"Then there's *this* business," says Dad, pointing down to the dog basket. Dudley has woken a little and is trying to lift his leg up to scratch his ear. It looks very funny to see a boy's trainer waving about like that instead of a paw.

Danny and Priya exchange glances.

Sausage rolls? Hosepipe? Four hundred pounds? None of this sounds good.

"Listen," says Priya hurriedly, "Dudley was such a star at the Doggy Boot Camp! He was the best dog there! And guess what? Rex Power thinks he should enter the dog show at the County Fair tomorrow!" Not strictly true but a necessary white lie.

"Hmm," says Dad, still frowning down at Dudley, "I don't know about that. We have enough going on right now to worry about dog shows."

"There's a big cash prize," says Priya with a twinkle in her eye. "And rumour has it that Cressida Cruickshank off the telly is the judge."

Dad's eyebrows shoot up. He and Mum look at each other.

"Cash prize?" says Mum.

"Yes," says Priya. "Enough to cover all the damage, with a hundred quid to spare!"

"Did you say 'Cressida Cruickshank'?" says Dad, looking distracted.

But Mum lets out a big sigh. "Nope," she says. "Dudley could never do it."

Danny paws at Priya's foot and gives a little whine.

He's going to have to show them.

He lies down, then rolls onto his back with all legs in the air like an upside-down hairy table. Then he gets up and resumes a neat sitting position, looking at everyone in turn.

They all stare at him curiously.

But Priya starts grinning. She gets what he's trying to do.

"Heel!" she says. Danny trots over to her and sits neatly at her feet.

"Fetch the toy!"

Danny trots over to Dudley's tuggy toy and lifts it in his mouth before coming back to lay it carefully at Priya's feet.

"Go and, um, I don't know, find an egg!" says Priya.

An egg?

"No!" Mum and Dad cry in unison, but Danny is already skidding into the kitchen in search of the chicken-shaped egg container near the kettle.

Standing on his hind legs, he delicately takes an egg in his mouth and carries it back into the hall.

Please don't break...

But he manages to gently drop the perfectly whole egg into Priya's waiting hands.

"See?" she says, beaming.

"My goodness," says Mum.

"He's like a different dog," says Dad. "That class has really paid off!"

Danny and Priya exchange glances. It's time to come clean and confess to Mum and Dad that it's happened again...

15

Dudley gives one of his happy stretches, all four legs at once. He's been sleeping on Danny's bed and *no one has told him off*. Doesn't really smell right though.

And he still misses Danny. Maybe he'll come back today! With this cheerful thought in his head, he pads down the stairs, past the Other Dog sleeping in his dog bed (hmm...) and goes into the kitchen.

The Dad is making something that smells very yummy indeed.

"Oh hello, um, Dudley—"

"DUDLEY!" barks Dudley, pleased to hear his name.

"Oh this is really going to take some getting used to," says the Dad. "My boy is a dog, and my dog is a boy. So I guess this bacon is for you?"

Dudley is so stunned he can't even bark, he just stands, gawping, in the middle of the kitchen.

For him? *All of it?*

The Mum comes into the room and stops dead.

"This is so weird," she says, peering at Dudley. "Now I know what's going on, I can see Dudley in there, can't you?"

"Yes," says the Dad. "It's something about the gormless expression on his face."

"Come on, then," says the Mum, "have your breakfast, Dudley. I'll wake my son and give him some kibble." She walks away muttering, "Can't believe I just said that."

The Dad gives Dudley the bacon sandwich one tiny piece at a time.

Once the sandwich is all gone, the Dad and the Mum come and sit at the table. Both have worried expressions.

"Right, Dudley," says the Mum. "Priya's coming over soon and then we're all going to the County Fair. All you have to do is to stay close all day, OK?"

Dudley can do **STAYING!** He barks his name again.

"We need you to be a good boy today," says the Dad. "Do you think you can do that?"

He can be the Good Boy!

So they understand, he barks his name over and over again until they both go a funny colour and tell him to stop.

Danny is in the very back of the car, fretting.

It looks like Dad is feeling tense too – about the cake competition. Mum is driving and Dad has cake boxes piled on his lap. Every time they turn a corner, he sucks in his breath and clutches the boxes tighter.

Dudley sits in front of him, wearing a seatbelt but not *quite* looking like a normal boy because his head is out of the window, his tongue is out,

and there's a daft, blissful expression on his face.

Danny cringes. What if someone from school sees him?

This is the thought that kept him awake almost all night and he only managed to doze for a little while this morning. So he's tired as well as worried.

And what if he isn't very good in the dog show? What if he lets everyone down?

Priya is next to Dudley. She turns from the back seat to look at him.

"All right, Danny?" she says. "Ready to win that prize money?"

He gulps. Is he? What if he can't do it? And what if Dudley misbehaves and everyone laughs? What if Dudley licks someone from school?

What if someone films it and puts it on the internet?

The thought makes his paws sweat. This could be a very long day.

17

Dudley doesn't normally like being in the vroom-vroom machine but that was fun! He was allowed to stick his head out of the window *all the way*.

After a while the car stops at a place where there is lots of GREEN and they all get out. It's like the park, but there are more humans around. And there are loads of other dogs. Dudley wants to go and sniff some bottoms, like he normally does on walkies, but he is being the

Good Boy and **STAYING**, like he was told to.

He wishes he could cover his hearing flappers with his paws though. There are shouty voices and big loud machines that go *hummmmm*. Then something goes **CRACK** so loudly that Dudley whimpers and presses himself close to the Priya. She pats his head and whispers, "It's all right, Dudders, it's just the rifle range."

The Other Dog starts to lick him and it makes him feel a bit better. Maybe the Other Dog isn't so bad after all, even though he doesn't smell right.

"Dudley hates loud noises," says the Dad. "I'm going to take him away while you do the dog show but I'll steer clear of the rifle range."

Dudley's soon distracted again because even with his broken sniff, there are so many yummy food smells. He starts to wander towards one with lovely meaty whiffs coming from it, but the Mum grabs one of his leggies and pulls him back.

"Now then, Dudley," she says. "Remember to *stay*!"

He's trying but it's very, very hard. Looking longingly back over his shoulder as they pass, he isn't paying attention to the pile of something soft that's in his way.

Oh dear. He falls right on top of it. It smells very bad indeed and just for a moment he wishes his sniff was even more broken.

"Oh my goodness," says the Dad. "Tell me that isn't a cowpat."

"Um, that isn't a cowpat," says the Priya.

"It is, though," says the Dad through gritted teeth. "It *is* a cowpat."

"Crikey," says the Mum, brushing at Dudley's leggies with her hand, her face all squinched. "I'm starting to wonder whether coming here was a terrible mistake!"

"Cheer up!" says the Priya. "There are prizes to be won!"

"That's true," says the Dad. "Cake tent, here I come!"

The Mum and the Priya look at each other.

But Dudley's got **CAKE** on his mind!

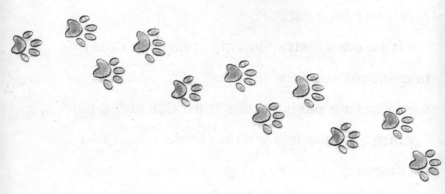

So many smells! Danny tries to identify each one to take his mind off his nerves.

Along with the usual people pongs, he's picked up:

1. Sugary candyfloss.

2. Hot, buttery popcorn.

3. Savoury, meaty hotdogs. (These make him drool! Embarrassing.)

4. The sharp smell of petrol from the fairground machines.

5. Stinky horse manure from the pony rides.

It's a good distraction but it doesn't quite take his mind off the fact that he has already seen eight people he knows from school.

Please keep a low profile, Dudders. Don't let me down...

At the "Pet Central – for all your animal's needs" Dog Show enclosure, Danny, Mum and Priya are taken to the competitors' area. Just like before, all the other dogs sense something wrong about him. There's a lot of rumbly growling and suspicious sniffing going on. It's not only dogs that know something is amiss either: when they walked past the petting zoo, a pot-bellied pig actually bared its teeth at him.

"Don't worry," says Priya, not very convincingly. "I'm sure it will be fine!"

A loud voice cuts through the air.

"Oh, what a simply marvellous pooch! May I?"

Danny turns to see a familiar face beaming down at him.

It's Cressida Cruickshank off the telly. She has a huge smile and lots of blonde hair that swishes in a similar way to Princess Fenella's. She sports a pair of sparkly sunglasses, which she takes off before crouching down in front of Danny.

"Who is this delightful creature?" she says, then touches Danny's nose and goes "BOOP!"

"Hi," says Priya. Mum looks a bit starstruck and doesn't say anything at all. "This is Dan— I mean Dudley! He's with us."

"He's such a beauty!" says Cressida. "I've never seen a dog with such an intelligent expression! It's like he understands *everything* we say!" Danny has to resist rolling his eyes at this. Of course he does! She gives his nose another

BOOP. "Aren't you a gorgeous boy then? Yes, you are! You are!" Grabbing him by both ears, she kisses the top of his head with big smacking sounds.

"Ms Cruickshank!" calls a woman with a clipboard. "We need you now."

Thank goodness. Danny has had quite enough kissing and booping.

Cressida Cruickshank gets up. "I'll see *you* later, you gorgeous boy!"

As she swishes away, Danny catches sight of Princess Fenella and Rex Power. Unlike yesterday though, she won't sit still. She tries to jump up at her glaring owner and then starts barking at the other dogs taking part. Most of them are barking at Danny.

But Fenella is the worst behaved of all! So much for "canine perfection"! It reminds Danny of that funny moment she had yesterday, but this is worse! If some of the Boot Camp people were here, they'd demand their money back!

After a few moments, Rex

Power leads her away behind one of the food stands. Danny can't see what he does, but when they come back, the dog is her snooty, perfectly behaved self again. Odd.

Anyway, they are all being called over for the first event.

"Greetings, everyone!" booms a beaming Cressida Cruickshank through a screeching microphone. "Welcome to this year's exciting dog show, sponsored by Pet Central, a grooming service for all your animal's needs! I can't wait to see what these clever pooches can do!"

This is it, thinks Danny. *No turning back now.*

19

Dudley is in heaven *again*. So many cakes! He stares dreamily at a table that's laden with delicious things. He has been a Very Good Boy so far and not eaten any of them. The Dad said so, although he keeps telling him to put his tongue back in his mouth, which is a bit silly if you ask Dudley.

"Just place your, um, offerings here on the table," says a smiley lady to the Dad, who

carefully puts his own cakes down next to some much, much bigger ones. "Judging's at three! In the meantime, would you and your son like a go at welly throwing? My wife is running that just next door!"

"Er, no," says the Dad quickly. "Thank you but we'll give that a miss! Come on, er, son!"

"Oh hey," says a voice. A boy the same size as Danny, but disappointingly *not* Danny, is standing next to him. Dudley wants to give him a sniff to check him out, but the Dad is firmly holding one of his leggies so he can't move.

"Boring, isn't it?" says the boy with a big yawn that shows all his teeth. "Mum won't let me do the mud wrestling, or have anything else to eat. I've only had some candyfloss, two toffee apples and three hot dogs, and now I fancy one of those fairy cakes over there."

DOGS? Dudley wants to woof but the Dad pulls him quickly so he almost falls over.

"Sorry, Danny's friend!" he says. "Gotta dash over to the dog show!"

Huh. Dudley didn't even get to hear more about the dogs that were hot.

Outside the big tent, the Dad tries to lead him away. But Dudley sees something that makes his eyes go very, very wide.

People are throwing shoes around.

People. Are. Throwing. Shoes.

Dudley likes eating shoes! And he likes people throwing things!

The Dad squawks, "**STOP!**" and something about "welly throwing!" but Dudley has important things on his mind.

"Let's see if your pooch can count!" says the commentator through the crackly speaker.

Now, maths isn't Danny's strongest subject, but he's fairly sure he's better at it than a whippet called Keith. That's who he's up against, along with a Shih Tzu named Muffin, a Border collie called Patrick and, of course, Princess Fenella.

The first round, an obedience test, has

already weeded out the
weakest candidates.
Lollipop the West Highland
terrier was disqualified
immediately for chewing

one of the plastic cones marking the way.

They get started. What Danny has to do is
paw the ground according to the number of times
the commentator blows a whistle.

One. *Paw...*

Two. *Paw, paw...*

Three. *Paw, paw, paw...*

So easy! But
the other dogs
must think so too
because all of them
get top marks –
apart from Keith
who gets none.

Keith is out.

Next comes the memory test. There's a series of identical cones, one of which has a treat inside it. The cones get moved around and the dog has to remember where the treat is.

It starts off OK but then Danny's concentration wavers. He's fretting about what Dudley is up to while in possession of his body and so he loses a couple of points. *Must concentrate!*

Princess Fenella is ahead of him now. He's level pegging with Muffin.

Patrick is out.

"It's time for our last challenge before we break for lunch," says the commentator with a few crackles. "We have the mini obstacle course.

This is a qualifying round for the big agility course later. Owners, please take your dogs to the starting line!"

"You'll smash this, Danny," says Priya, grinning, as they run over together.

And he does.

Danny sails through the course and gets a perfect ten points. This time he even manages to do *two* backflips on the trampoline. It's like his boy-brain, combined with his doggy body, have given him superpowers. Watching those parkour videos has paid off and it's even better with four legs!

Cressida Cruickshank, watching from the guest-of-honour judging table, gives a loud "WHOOP!"

Princess Fenella gets a nine.

Muffin is out.

It's a dead heat now between Danny and Princess Fenella, whose owner is glowering at him from across the way.

"Time for some lunch, people!" says the commentator through the speaker "Then we'll have the grand finale – the agility course! Let's see how our two clever finalists get on!"

Danny is only one step away from winning £500.

Mum and Dad will be so happy about the prize money that they might cut Dudley a bit of slack. He might even get to sleep on Danny's bed ALL the time! And there will be no more talk of sending him to horrible Doggy Boot Camp.

He wags his tail happily. This might turn out really well, after all!

21

"STOP EATING THAT WELLY, YOUNG MAN!"

A shouty lady with a long nose towers over Dudley. He's lying on the ground, trying to chew one of the funny shoes. It's too hard, though, which is surprising when chewing is one of the things Dudley is best at.

Lots of people are looking at him. The Dad has both his paws over his eyes. Hiding? Dudley loves a hiding game! But chewing shoes is better.

"**PLEASE REMOVE YOUR SON IMMEDIATELY!**" shouts the lady. The shoutyness is scary and Dudley whimpers.

"Of course! Of course!" says the Dad. "I'm so sorry. He's, er, not feeling himself today! Come on, boy… I mean Danny!"

He lifts Dudley up from the ground by one his front leggies. Dudley is still holding onto the shoe with his teeth.

"I SAID PUT THAT WELLY DOWN!" The lady's voice is hurting Dudley's hearing flappers. Dudley whimpers and then there's a big **CRACK!** nearby.

Dudley hates **CRACKS!**

Looking around wildly, he can see some people with long sticks. They're pointing them into the sky and making them go **CRACK! CRACK! CRACK!**

Too loud! Got to get away!

"Come back here!" yells the Dad.

Instead, Dudley runs. And runs.

22

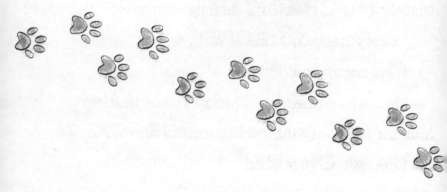

Danny hears someone say, "There's a boy causing havoc over there! No one can catch him!"

Danny and Priya look at each other. Mum and Danny look at each other. Mum and Priya look at each other.

They're all thinking the same thing:

DUDLEY!

Danny whines.

He wants to say, "What the heck is Dudley *doing*? This is so *embarrassing*," but a whine is all he has.

Rex Power, watching them, sidles over.

"Everything OK?" he says in an oily voice. "You look rather worried."

"No, we're fine," says Mum. "I just need to go and, um, help my husband with something."

"I've got an idea," says Power with a slow grin. "Why don't I take Dudley over to have lunch with Princess Fenella? I give her only the very best dog food, for maximum performance. Might help Dudley in that final challenge!"

Mum only hesitates for a moment.

"Thank you, Mr Power," she says. "That's very kind of you."

"No problem," says Rex Power. "I'll bring him back soon."

Something about this feels off. But Danny is worried, embarrassed and actually really, really hungry. We're talking Dudley levels of hungry. So, a bit cautiously, he follows the trainer away and across to a different field.

They go to a big white trailer, with *REX POWER – EXTREME DOG TRAINER*™ written on the side. Power glowers down at Danny behind his shiny glasses and lays down bowls of food for him and Princess Fenella.

Princess Fenella regards Danny, lifting one shivery lip in a low growl that makes Danny feel nervous in his tummy. Maybe she thinks he's going to steal her lunch. (Tempting.)

Power gives Danny a strange, slow smile. "It's important, don't you think," he says, "that every dog gets what it deserves?" He pats Princess Fenella's head. "Isn't that right, my princess?"

Bit weird, but Danny is so hungry he devours the delicious meaty dog food, then licks the bowl until all that's left is the shine.

Rex Power looks around quickly as if checking for something, then squats down on his haunches to Danny's level.

"Good dog," he says. "Now why don't you take a little look at this?" From his pocket he produces a big gold watch on a chain. Instead of hands, there are two dog bones, and instead of numbers, there are twelve tiny images of Rex Power himself, complete with shades.

The man starts to swing the watch to and fro, to and fro...

Danny can't seem to keep his eyes off it.

Soon his limbs feel heavy and everything looks like wibbly-wobbly lines. He gives a wide yawn.

He's ... so ... very ... sleepy...

The sun glinting off Power's sunglasses and teeth are the last thing he sees before everything goes dark.

23

Shouty voices everywhere! Dudley jumps over a
fence to escape as a man with an angry face says,
"You can't go in there, lad! That's the agility
course for the dogs!"

Dogs? That must mean he's allowed! Maybe
people will stop shouting at him now? But he can't
see any dogs and someone is still yelling, so he
keeps running. There are lots of big **THINGS**
in his way and he crashes about in his panic.

He jumps over some and sends others toppling down around him. When he reaches the fence at the top, he crashes straight through it.

But now he's in an *even worse* place! Huge, gleaming monsters with big teeth and wild eyes snort at him through their long noses.

"NEIGH!" say the monsters. "NEIGH!" More hot snortiness comes from their noses. Their funny paws go *clop-clop-clop* on the ground. They want to trample Dudley all over!

GOT TO GET AWAY!

But there's nowhere to run! He's suddenly surrounded by humans, including the Mum, the Dad and the Priya.

"Oh dear, oh dear," says someone. "Whatever has this boy done?"

"We're so sorry!" says the Dad, his face as red as Dudley's favourite chewy ball.

"Remember the whole 'staying' thing?" hisses the Priya.

The Mum says nothing. She puts her paws over her face.

Seems like everyone is playing the hiding game today.

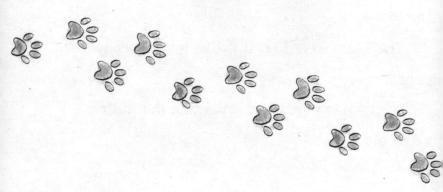

Danny is dreaming about bones.

Bones swimming around in the air. Bones in a swirly kaleidoscope of every colour.

Bones on a watch face.

Huh?

His eyes snap open and he lifts his head. He's on a bed in what looks like Rex Power's trailer, judging from the many framed pictures of him with Fenella, plus a whole shelf of products with

names like "Fake Tan for REAL Men".

What's he doing in here?

Danny thinks about the tiny bones on the watch face. Then it all makes sense.

Rex Power hypnotized him using that special pocket watch! Maybe that's how he gets naughty dogs to behave. What a big fraud!

Danny jumps off the bed and it's only as his paws skid to the door of the trailer that he realizes he has no way of opening it.

How he misses having thumbs!

He's stuck. There's only one thing he can do...

Danny starts to bark. It's the loudest, barkiest bark he can muster. And it's all he's got.

25

The humans have been standing around for ages, talking in cross voices. No one has given Dudley his lunch. And there hasn't been one single treat!

Dudley has had enough. He lies down on the ground and tries to curl up small.

But the Dad isn't happy about that either.

"Get up, you daft dog!" he says. "Honestly! Eating wellies? Running away from horses? Scared of the junior rifle range?" He sighs.

"Can't you be more like, well, Danny?"

Danny? Where *is* Danny? It seems like everyone is having the same thought because the Mum says, "Actually, where is Danny? Mr Power said he would bring him back after a quick bite to eat."

"It has been a while," says the Priya. "Do you think everything's OK?"

At that moment, Rex Power runs up.

"We have a problem!" he says. "I'm afraid your dog proved to be rather uncontrollable and ran off as soon as we got to my trailer! I've been looking for him everywhere!"

"Oh no!" says the Dad.

The Mum puts her paws to her cheeks and her eyes go wide. "He could be anywhere!" she says. "Let's split up and look. Dudley, you keep close to Priya, OK?"

The humans start to move away but Dudley stays where he is, hearing flappers turned in the other direction.

Because he can hear something...

It's a very special sort of dog bark. It is, in fact, the very best dog bark going. Why does Dudley know this?

Because *it's his own bark.*

Some dog has stolen his bark!

He doesn't understand why or how this has happened. But he has to find that dog and get it back!

Danny has almost barked himself hoarse.

How is he going to get out of here?

After what seems ages, he hears a familiar voice.

"Where are you *going?* Don't you think you've caused enough trouble for one day?"

It's Mum! And...

"Dudley! Dudley!" says a funny growly voice.

Dudley! Phew!

"Danny! Where are you?" Priya's here too.

"We can't waste time!" says Dad. "We have to find him! Mr Power says he ran away from here!"

That lying...

Danny digs deep for the loudest bark yet.

"Dudley! Dudley! I'm in here! I'm in here!"

27

The dog who stole his bark is **INSIDE** the big white box on wheels! Why can't they hear?

The scary man with the shiny eyes runs up with his own dog, the one with long swishy hair, who growls at Dudley.

Dudley would normally be scared but he is feeling brave! He is defending his bark.

"What are you doing by my trailer?" says the man crossly. Then he sees a lady with hair just like the man's dog coming up behind him.

"Ah, Cressida!" he says and sounds quite different now.

"Rex," she says, "you simply must get a move on! We're about to do the final challenges!"

She looks at the Mum, the Dad and the Priya.

"And where is your doggy? Hmm? It's not on, I mean really! I'm not getting paid enough for all these delays!"

"I think he's in there," says the Priya, pointing to the big shiny box.

Another distinctive bark comes from inside.

"That really sounds like him!" says the Priya.

"I agree!" says the Mum. "Open the trailer!"

"Well, I really don't see why I should have to," says the scary Rex man.

"Open the trailer!" says the Dad.

"Rex!" says the dog-hair lady. "*Do it!*"

The scary Rex man hesitates for a few moments and then opens the big white box on wheels, grumbling the whole time.

That Other Dog from before shoots out, almost knocking him over.

"Oh," says the scary Rex man. "However did you get in there, you silly thing?"

"Don't call him silly," says the Priya, then, "Hang on, what's he got in his mouth?"

The Other Dog drops something at her feet and looks up expectantly.

"What's this, Danny?" she whispers, picking it up.

"Give me that!" The scary Rex man tries to snatch it from the Priya but she dodges him and holds it up.

"Let me see!" says the dog-hair lady.

"I know what this is," she says, taking it from the Priya. "I've seen this before at another dog show." She puts her hands on her hips and confronts the scary Rex man. "You're hypnotizing dogs into doing what you want, aren't you?"

Dudley doesn't know what all this shouting is about. He wishes they would stop.

He just wants his bark back. But no one is paying attention to him because they are all looking at the dog that doesn't like Dudley instead. Something's happening. She's watching the thing in the lady's hand go back and forth...

... back and forth...

Then she collapses in a heap and starts snoring.

"Lady Fenella was looking at the watch!" says the Priya. "That proves it!"

"You're bang to rights, Rex Power!" says the Mum.

"You're disqualified, Rex Power!" says the dog-hair lady.

Danny is exhausted.

It's been quite the day! He won the dog show because he was the only remaining contestant. But who cares why? He can feel the shiny medal go *clink-clink* against his collar. Danny's looking forward to reminding Mum and Dad about that medal when Dudley misbehaves.

Best not to think about the people who saw him – or rather Dudley – at the County Fair though. He looks at his dog, sitting in front of him, still in possession of Danny's own boy-body.

Dudley is obviously getting sleepy. He sways with the movement of the car, a soppy, faraway look on his face as he gazes out of the window.

Mum's trying to make Dad feel better about not getting anywhere in the baking competition. It seems his banana bread fell off the table and injured a judge's big toe.

"But it wasn't *broken* or anything," says Mum. "Just, er, badly bruised. So it could be worse?"

"I think the problem is that I haven't practised enough," says Dad thoughtfully. "Maybe I just need to try harder. Do lots more baking?"

Mum meets Danny's eye in the rear-view mirror and makes a funny, horrified face.

He wishes he could do a proper boy-laugh in return.

Meanwhile, Dudley sways in front of him ...

... lunges at Priya in a hug, and then lays his head on her lap, spark out.

Priya turns to look back at Danny, her hands up in the air.

"Argh!" she says. "This is weird!"

Danny can cope with seeing himself do all sorts of things, but snuggling up to his cousin is going too far!

Surely the magic has worn off again now? Got to be worth trying to wish them back himself? Danny closes his doggy eyes as tightly as they can go and thinks, *I wish, I WISH I was back in my boy-body.* Nothing.

I WISH, I WISH I WAS BACK IN MY BOY-BODY! He does it one more time to be sure and then ...

... there's a yappy *whooshing* and ...

... he's lying on Priya's lap. He sits bolt upright in about a nanosecond. Priya, wide-eyed, stares at him.

"Phew," says Danny. "I'm back!"

Dudley, behind him, gives a happy "WOOF!" Which Danny thinks almost certainly means, "Me too!"

29

Dudley wakes up in his own doggy bed, feeling happy. Danny's bed was nice but he'd been missing the special smell of his own.

And the best thing is, Danny's back!

He appeared in the vroom-vroom machine *right in front of Dudley's eyes* yesterday. When they got out, he bent down and gave Dudley the biggest, squeeziest hug ever and said, "I'm so happy to see you, boy. Look, I've got a present for you!"

Then he tapped something that went *clink-clink* against Dudley's collar.

"This is a Good Boy Medal," said Danny, looking into Dudley's eyes. "It was given to me, but you won it really because you saved the day."

A GOOD BOY MEDAL?

Now Dudley doesn't really know what a medal is. But he's the Good Boy! Finally everyone agrees!

He lifts his head now and hears the *clink-clink*, which makes him sigh with contentment. Still the Good Boy!

What's more, a delicious smell drifts up his nose. The Dad appears at the kitchen door.

"Guys?" he calls out. "I think I might have cracked this cake recipe now! It's not *quite* as heavy as yesterday's! Does anyone want to try it?"

"Guys?" says the Dad. "Anyone?"

Cake?

Dudley goes over and sits so close, his front paws are on the Dad's feet. He looks up. Slowly, the Dad looks down and meets his gaze. They stare at each other for several moments, human and dog, locked in silent eye battle.

"Oh, I give up," says the Dad with a big sigh. "Come on then," he says, "I guess you can have one *small* piece. Seeing as you're my biggest fan and everything. And you have a medal."

Dudley wags his tail so hard his whole body sways from side to side.

Now he's the Good Boy, he's allowed to have all the cake he wants!

He can see it, sitting right there on the table. All for him!

Dudley runs into the kitchen, knocking over a chair on the way. As he leaps towards the freshly baked cake, mouth open and ready to devour it, the Dad goes:

"DUDLEY, NOOOOO!"

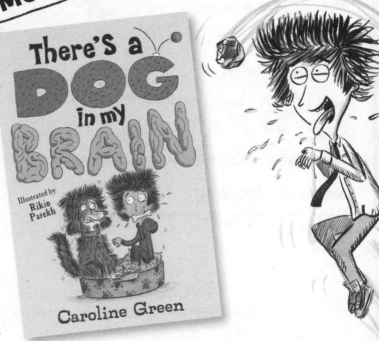

WARNING

MORE CANINE COMEDY CHAOS

There's a DOG in my BRAIN

Illustrated by Rikin Parekh

Caroline Green

When Danny makes a wish to stay at home instead of going to a family wedding, he doesn't expect to swap places with his dog, Dudley. Now he's trapped in the body of a dog – and Dudley is trapped in the body of a ten-year-old boy!

This surprise body swap is about to get both of them into Very Big Trouble...